First Facts®

Positively Pets

Caring for Your
Bird

by June Preszler

Consultant:
Jennifer Zablotny, DVM
Member, American Veterinary Medical Association

Capstone
press®

Mankato, Minnesota

First Facts is published by Capstone Press,
151 Good Counsel Drive, P.O. Box 669, Mankato, Minnesota 56002.
www.capstonepress.com

Library of Congress Cataloging-in-Publication Data
Preszler, June, 1954–
    Caring for your bird/by June Preszler.
    p. cm. — (First facts. Positively pets)
    Summary: "Simple text and photographs discuss ways to take care of pet birds" — Provided
by publisher.
    Includes bibliographical references and index.
    ISBN-13: 978-1-4296-1252-4 (hardcover)
    ISBN-10: 1-4296-1252-5 (hardcover)
    1. Cage birds — Juvenile literature. I. Title. II. Series.
SF461.35.P74 2008
636.6'8 — dc22   2007024199

Editorial Credits
Gillia Olson and Megan Schoeneberger, editors; Bobbi J. Wyss, set designer; Kyle Grenz, book
    designer and illustrator; Kelly Garvin, photo researcher/photo stylist

Photo Credits
All photos Capstone Press/Karon Dubke, except page 20, Shutterstock/William Attard McCarthy

Capstone Press thanks Tiffani and Cory Atherton of Elysian, Minnesota, for use of their wonderful
    birds and location. Thank you also to Pet Expo in Mankato, Minnesota, for assistance in photo
    shoots for this book.

1 2 3 4 5 6 13 12 11 10 09 08

Table of Contents

Do You Want a Bird?

Birds can be great pets. Birds are smart, cheerful, and noisy. Some birds sing or chirp. Others even **mimic** your words.

Birds need you to share time with them and care for them. Before getting a bird, make sure you are ready to care for your new friend.

I'm a budgie, although some people call me a parakeet. I make a great pet. Cockatiels and canaries can be good pets too.

Supplies to Buy

A pet bird needs a safe, roomy cage with cups for food and water. The cage should have **perches** or branches where birds can **roost**.

Birds like to play. Small birds peek into mirrors. Large birds enjoy metal rings and chew toys. Some birds like ladders or swings.

How about getting me some upbeat tunes? I like to dance and move my body to the beat of the music.

7

Your Bird at Home

Your bird needs time to feel safe. Talk to it softly in its cage. Once a bird feels at home, you can let it perch on your finger or arm. Shoulder rides are not a good idea. Even small birds could peck your face. Shoulder sitting may be possible later with small birds. Large birds might never be shoulder riders.

Hey, I'm ticklish! We birds enjoy getting our necks tickled.

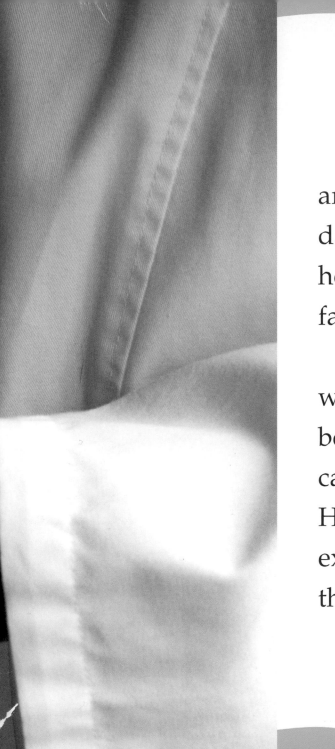

Letting your bird fly around the house can be dangerous. Other pets, hot stoves, and ceiling fans can hurt birds.

Trimming a bird's wings allows it to be safe outside of its cage. It can't fly away. Have a **veterinarian** or experienced adult do the trimming.

Feeding Your Bird

Different birds need different foods to be healthy. Most bird food should include **pellets** mixed with a few nuts. Birds can also eat small amounts of people foods. Bird favorites are seeds, leafy greens, fruits, yogurt, and cheese. All birds need fresh water daily.

If a food is good for people, it's probably good for me. Sometimes I even like a little bit of spaghetti!

Keeping a Healthy Bird

A clean cage helps your pet stay healthy. Each day, clean the bottom of the cage. Each week, clean the whole cage and the bird's toys.

Every year, take your bird to a **veterinarian** for a checkup. The vet can talk about your bird's care and its health and food needs.

Your Bird and Other Pets

Your bird can get along with other pets, but be careful. Dogs and cats like to hunt birds. You'll have to teach other pets not to hurt your bird.

Another bird is the best animal friend for your bird. Some birds get lonely without a bird buddy.

Your Bird's Life

The larger the pet bird, the longer it can live. Some cockatoos can live up to 65 years. Canaries, budgies, and cockatiels live between 10 and 20 years. No matter how long your bird lives, it will always need your care and love.

About 200 years ago, people began to catch parrots and keep them as pets. Until then, parrots lived in the wild. Parrots' wild relatives still live out in nature. Today, most pet birds come from people who raise them from babies. That way, wild birds get to stay wild.

Decode Your Bird's Behavior

- If it stops eating, talking, or playing, your bird might be sick.

- A noisy or talking bird usually means a happy bird. Pet birds that feel safe like to make noise.

- Birds flap their wings for many reasons. Sometimes pet birds fly in place for exercise. Other times birds flap their wings to get your attention.

- Dogs aren't the only pets that wag their tails. Birds may wag their tails to show they're happy to see their owners.

- Yuck! Your bird just vomited in its cage. Is it sick? Probably not. Budgies and cockatiels show they are bonded with you by trying to share their food.

Glossary

mimic (MIM-ik) — to copy the look, actions, or behaviors of another animal

pellet (PEL-it) — a small, hard piece of food; pellets give birds the nutrition they need.

perch (PURCH) — a bar or branch on which a bird can rest

roost (ROOST) — a place where birds can sit, rest, or build nests

veterinarian (vet-ur-uh-NER-ee-uhn) — a doctor who treats sick or injured animals; veterinarians also help animals stay healthy.

Read More

Blackaby, Susan. *A Bird for You: Caring for Your Bird.* Pet Care. Minneapolis: Picture Window Books, 2003.

Phillips, Meredith. *Bird World.* Pet's Point of View. Minneapolis: Compass Point Books, 2005.

Rawson, Katherine. *If You Were a Parrot.* Mt. Pleasant, S.C.: Sylvan Dell, 2006.

Internet Sites

FactHound offers a safe, fun way to find Internet sites related to this book. All of the sites on FactHound have been researched by our staff.

Here's how:

1. Visit *www.facthound.com*

2. Choose your grade level.

3. Type in this book ID **1429612525** for age-appropriate sites. You may also browse subjects by clicking on letters, or by clicking on pictures and words.

4. Click on the **Fetch It** button.

FactHound will fetch the best sites for you!

Index